MW01048415

This book belongs to

_____

The Three Billy Goats Gruff

RETOLD BY

Jennifer Greenway

ILLUSTRATED BY

Loretta Lustig

ARIEL BOOKS

ANDREWS AND McMEEL
KANSAS CITY

Library of Congress Cataloging-in-Publication Data

Greenway, Jennifer.
     The three billy goats Gruff / retold by Jennifer Greenway ; illustrated by
Loretta Lustig.
        p.   cm.
     "Ariel books."
     Adaptation of Peter Christen Asbjørnsen's Tre bukkene Bruse.
     Summary: Three clever billy goats outwit a big, ugly troll that lives
under the bridge they must cross on their way up the mountain.
     ISBN 0-8362-4913-5 : $6.95
     [1. Fairy tales. 2. Folklore—Norway.] I. Lustig, Loretta, ill.
II. Asbjørnsen, Peter Christen, 1812–1885. Tre bukkene Bruse. III. Title.
PZ8.G84Th   1991
398.2—dc20
     [E]   91–17523
                                                                   CIP
                                                                    AC
10 9 8 7 6 5 4 3

Design: Susan Hood and Mike Hortens
Art Direction: Armand Eisen, Mike Hortens, and Julie Phillips
Art Production: Lynn Wine

The Three
Billy Goats Gruff

Once upon a time there were three billy goats. The name of these three goats was Gruff, so they were known as the Three Billy Goats Gruff.

The Three Billy Goats Gruff lived in a rocky field at the bottom of a grassy hill. The grass in this field was brown and tough, and the Three Billy Goats Gruff were always hungry.

The Three Billy Goats Gruff wished they could go up the hill to where the grass was green and tender. "If we could only do that," they said, "then we would all become fat and be very happy."

However, to get up the hill, the Three Billy Goats Gruff had to cross a bridge that went over a rushing stream. Under this bridge, there lived a big ugly troll who liked nothing better than to eat billy goats and anything else that crossed his path.

So the Three Billy Goats Gruff stayed where they were. But every day they looked up at the hillside and sighed, for they so longed to go there and enjoy the tender grass.

One day, the youngest Billy Goat Gruff turned to his brothers and said, "I can't bear trying to chew this tough brown grass anymore. I am going to go up the hillside to where the grass is green and sweet!"

"But what about the troll?" exclaimed the other two. "He will surely eat you up!"

"Perhaps he will," the youngest Billy Goat Gruff replied. "But if I stay in this field, I will surely starve anyway! I am going to cross that bridge."

"But you are the smallest of us all!" said the other Billy Goats Gruff. "The troll will be able to eat you with no trouble!"

"We shall see about that," said the youngest Billy Goat Gruff.

So off the youngest Billy Goat Gruff went. When he reached the bridge where the troll lived he started across it as fast as he could. *Tip-tap, tip-tap, tip-tap* went his tiny little hooves.

The big ugly troll heard something overhead, and just as the youngest Billy Goat Gruff reached the center of the bridge, the troll called out in his big voice:

"Who's that crossing my bridge?"

"It's only me," replied the youngest Billy Goat Gruff in his tiny little voice.

"Is that so?" roared the troll. "Well, I am going to eat you up!"

The youngest Billy Goat Gruff was very frightened, but he replied bravely, "Oh, please don't do that. I am so small and thin, I would hardly be enough for a snack for such a big creature as you."

"You'll do fine," the troll said.

"No," cried the youngest Billy Goat Gruff. "Wait until my brother, the second Billy Goat Gruff, comes along. He is much bigger and fatter than I. He will make you a much better supper!"

The troll was quite hungry, so he agreed to wait.

The youngest Billy Goat Gruff continued on his way—*tip-tap, tip-tap, tip-tap*—up the hillside to where the grass grew green and thick. There, the youngest Billy Goat Gruff ate to his heart's content, and he began to grow fat.

After a while, the second Billy Goat Gruff decided he would try his luck. So off he went toward the bridge where the troll lived. When he reached the bridge he started across it as fast as he could. *Trip-trap, trip-trap, trip-trap* went his middle-sized hooves. The troll heard him and cried in his big voice, "Who's that crossing my bridge?"

"It's only me," replied the second Billy Goat Gruff in his middle-sized voice.

"Is that so?" said the troll. "Well, I am going to eat you up!"

The second Billy Goat Gruff was very frightened, but he replied bravely, "Oh, no! Don't do that. I'm not nearly big and fat enough to satisfy such a big fellow like you. Wait until my brother, the third Billy Goat Gruff, comes along. He's much bigger than I, and I'm sure that he will fill you up!"

The troll, who was very hungry by now, agreed to wait once more.

So the second Billy Goat Gruff continued across the bridge—*trip-trap, trip-trap, trip-trap*—and soon he joined his younger brother on the hillside where the grass grew green and sweet.

The second Billy Goat Gruff ate and ate, and before long he was even fatter than his brother.

Now the third Billy Goat Gruff found himself all alone in the dry brown field. He decided to try his luck, too.

So off went the third Billy Goat Gruff toward the bridge where the troll lived.

When the third Billy Goat Gruff reached the bridge, he started across it as fast as he could. *TRAMP, TRAMP, TRAMP* went his big hooves. The big ugly troll heard him, and he cried out in his great big voice, "Who's that crossing my bridge?"

Then the troll poked his head up over the bridge to take a look. When the third Billy Goat Gruff saw him, he thought, "Why, that troll's not so big!" And he replied in his biggest voice, "It's only ME!"

"Is that so?" roared the troll. "Well, I'm going to eat you!"

"Let's see you try it," replied the third Billy Goat Gruff. And then he shouted:

I've got two big sharp horns
that will make you sore!
And two big pronged hooves
that will break your bones!
And lots of big sharp teeth
that will bite you all over!

Now, the troll was so hungry by this time that when he heard what the third Billy Goat said, he got mad! He jumped up onto the bridge and ran straight toward the third Billy Goat Gruff, shouting, "I'm going to eat you up right now!"

So the third Billy Goat Gruff butted the ugly troll with his big sharp horns. Then he kicked the troll with his big pronged hooves. Then he bit him all over with his big sharp teeth.

At last, the troll begged him to stop. "I promise I won't eat you!" he said. "Please, let me go!"

But the third Billy Goat Gruff kept on butting and kicking and biting him until, at last, the big ugly troll jumped off the bridge and was swept away by the rushing stream.

Then the third Billy Goat Gruff continued on his way—*TRAMP, TRAMP, TRAMP*—and soon he reached the hillside where the grass grew thick and green.

There he joined his brothers, and he ate and ate the tender grass and became very, very fat, which made him very, very happy.

So the three Billy Goats Gruff lived on the green hillside, and they all grew fatter and fatter. And for all I know they still live there today.

As for the big ugly troll, no one ever saw or heard of him again!